# The Last of Summer's Flowers

## A Tale of Hardship

By: JJ Krupitzer

Proofread and Edited By: Jaclyn Koffler

The Last of Summer's Flowers

Table of Contents:

Introduction

Hi there, everyone. It's nice to see you all again. As always, my name is JJ Krupitzer, and I'm here to spin you another tale. Surprisingly "The Last of Summer's Flowers" has nothing to do with an actual flower. The flower is used as a metaphor to describe our protagonist, Miss Charlie Manson. She is the "flower" so to speak. She has suffered many hardships throughout her life. Drugs, custody battles, losing her father, and so much more. So if you read this book and then look at the title and think it doesn't make sense, if you really look at all the hardships that she has gone through, it might make some sense. When I say "The Last of Summer's Flowers" I am not talking about an actual flower. I'm talking about the fragile balance of hardship, and trying to find your way through it. Again, that's what the "flower" part is. Anyway, hope you enjoy it! ~ JJ

Hello folks, my name is Charlie Manson. Now, now, now, before you get all in a tizzy, I'm not that crazy, and I am on the other side of the ball (I'm a girl). I was born to Dennis and Charlotte Manson on February 9, 1968, at 1:45 AM. I was born in Johnstown, Pennsylvania. My parents were originally from Wilmington, Delaware and moved to Johnstown, Pennsylvania in 1966 after getting married that same year. In 1967, they had my brother and sister, Alex and Alexa. Then, as I said before, I came along. They named me Charlie after my great grandfather. And before you ask, no he wasn't Charles Manson either. God, I can't tell you how many times I get asked that question on a daily basis. Anyway, let me stop rambling.

My mother was a seamstress's assistant, while my father worked as a bartender at a local bar. My parents had been married for about a year before I came along, actually two years, I'm sorry. I never saw them fight that much, and I knew that they loved each other very much. I didn't start seeing a discrepancy in the family fabric until 1971 when I was about three years old, that's when things really went to crap. It wasn't the fact of anyone drinking in the house or anything like that, my parents just weren't compatible anymore. Since I was the youngest, I began to blame myself for what had happened with my parents. My mother and father both told me not to worry about what was going on, sometimes mommies and daddies just don't work well together.

On August 19, 1971, my dad put a suitcase in front of the front door and put on a fedora along with his trenchcoat. "Well baby girl, daddy has to go away for a while. However, daddy will come visit you whenever I can." I began to cry because I didn't want my daddy to go. "Don't worry about it, my love, we will be ok on our own. We are strong and independent women, aren't we love bug?" I nodded my head yes, but my eyes were still filled with tears. "Oh now, don't cry Charlie, daddy will be back soon, before you know it in fact!" My mother reassured me, hoping to calm me down. Daddy came around about twice a week, then once a week, then once every two weeks, then once a month, then once every two months, and eventually, not at all!


"Mommy, where's daddy? Why doesn't he come around anymore, what did you do?" I asked sharply. She looked shocked that I wouldn't blame her for daddy not coming around. "Look, sweetie, I can't control what your dad does. If he wants to come around, he will come around. If he doesn't, then there is nothing I can do. I know you're not happy about this, but right now I can only be by myself and that's the best I can do for you. I'm sorry it's not what you want my darling." Two years go by, I still have not seen my father. My mother went to Ohio State from 1972 until 1976 to get a degree in private investigating. With her degree in 76, she was able to find my father and learn that he had moved to Cincinnati, Ohio and started a new family. My mother was devastated, I was devastated. My mother sat and cried into her hands, wondering what she did wrong.

I snuggled up next to my mother and reassured her that she did nothing wrong, and that daddy was a jerk. I was about eight years old when my father decided to be a scumbag. " mama, I will never forgive daddy for what he did to us!" My mother told me not to harbor harsh feelings for my father. He made a choice and he chose another woman, and sometimes that's okay. I didn't think it was okay, but if my mother did, there was nothing I could do. I was nine years old and didn't go to school because my mother could not afford it. We were so poor that we couldn't even get grants for me to go to school in the special education system. I have down syndrome. Down Syndrome or Down's Syndrome, also known as Trisomy 21, is a genetic disorder caused by the presence of all or part of a third copy of chromosome 21.It is usually associated with physical growth delays, mild to moderate intellectual disability, and characteristic facial features. The average IQ of a young adult with Down Syndrome is 50, equivalent to the mental ability of an eight- or nine-year-old child, but this can vary widely.

Finally in 1978, when I was 10, I got my big break, but this was because we moved to Honolulu, Hawaii and met a man by the name of Stephen Kekoa. Mr. Kekoa was a teacher of special needs children such as myself. As it is listed above, they say that the mental capacity of someone with Down Syndrome like myself, is about eight or nine years old. I guess I broke the mold so to speak, because my mental capacity was up there with everybody else's. I also met my first real friend when I was in Honolulu, Christina Lawson. Christina had cerebral palsy and used a wheelchair to motor around everywhere. Even though the school was filled with children that have special needs, we weren't free from bullies. Yes, people with disabilities bully other people with disabilities as well.

That's when I saw him, a 14 year old tall drink of water by the name of Luke Kekoa. Even though he was four years my senior, I never looked at anyone the way I looked at him, from the first moment I saw him. There was a little snag in my plan, we had to hurry back to Pennsylvania, because my mother had found out that my dad was in a horrible car accident and they were thinking about performing surgery, but they weren't sure the surgery would be a success, so we had to say our goodbyes in case it wasn't. "Mommy, why do we have to go back? He left us, it's not like he gave a crap about us, why should we give a crap about him?" That's when my mom slapped me across the face. "How dare you speak that way about your father, you should always be there for your family!" I rubbed my face because it was painful and I told my mother that I wasn't going with her back to Pennsylvania. I liked it perfectly fine where I was. She told me that she didn't care what I wanted, she was doing what was best for the family.

I cried my eyes out the whole way to the airport and begged my mother to let me stay. She said no, and that was the end of the conversation. We arrived at St. John's Hospital a few hours later, and I must admit, my dad was in pretty bad shape. "Charlotte, my darling, please come closer. I need to see your beautiful face one last time. I'm sorry for what I've done and I wish I could change things!" my father said to my mother. He wanted to say his peace to me, but I didn't want to hear anything he had to say. I sat there in the back of the room, sulking like there was no tomorrow. "Charlie, you get over here, you say goodbye to your father right now!" I refused, and that's when he coded. I heard the beeping and then flatline. When I heard the flat line, I'm not going to lie, I smiled. I know, I know, I should not have laughed at my father's demise but I think he deserved it. While my mom, brother, and sister all cried for my father, I felt at peace. This was because I firmly believed that there was nobody that was going to hurt my mother ever again.

As insensitive as it may sound, even at my fathers funeral, I did not shed one tear for the man. I couldn't, I couldn't shed tears for a man who hurt my family so much. I couldn't shed tears for a man who decided to leave my family in exchange for another one, I couldn't shed tears for a man who treated his second family better than his first one. His new wife and daughters were there, they offered their condolences to me and I just shrugged it off like it was nothing. "Eh, It's okay, it's a part of life. Nothing we can do about it. I will miss him, but God wanted him more than I did." His family looked at me strangely and walked away. I heard one of my stepsisters, and by stepsister's I use the term very loosely, but I heard one of my stepsister's call me a freak of nature, and she could understand why my father had left us. That was the first time that you could see any type of rage come out of me. I whipped around, I marched towards Peggy Sue, and I clocked her a good one right in the face.

"How dare you call me a freak, how dare you come near me and my family!" I yelled, causing a scene. "Charlie, please, calm down! This is not the time nor the place for one of your little tantrums!" My mother said to me, as she was pulling me off of Peggy Sue. Once Peggy Sue had gotten up, she had hocked a big spit wad in my face. When I went to go after her, my mother held me back and told me that was enough from me, and slapped my bottom once. On the drive home, my mother didn't say one word to me, but the look on her face, I could see from the mirror on the driver's side, it was a look of disappointment and great sadness. Finally when we pulled in the driveway, she spoke. "I can't believe you would embarrass me and the rest of our family like that at the funeral, what the hell were you thinking Charlie? Do you Not have any respect for your father at all, after all he had done for you?" Well, needless to say I felt about an inch big and I quickly apologized to my mother, brother, and sister for my actions.

I had asked my mother if we were going back to Honolulu again anytime soon so I could see Mr. Kekoa and his son. "No Charlie, I am so sorry, but I got a job offer here in Johnstown and I'm going to take it! "I wined and dined to go back to Honolulu, but it didn't work. My mother was dead set on staying in Johnstown. I didn't realize I would never see my precious Luke again, and I was greatly saddened by that fact. Luckily for me, my mother had gotten Mr. Kekoa's home address, and I was able to write to Luke almost every week. At first things were going great. I would hear from Luke weekly, then biweekly, then every three weeks, then every month and eventually, not at all. By 1981 the letters had stopped coming altogether. I slipped into a deep depression because I really liked Luke, I didn't understand why he didn't like me back. My mother could tell how much I was hurting and she told me not to worry about it, she told me that there were many other men that would be happy to have me in their lives. Of course, I didn't want to believe her. I wanted Luke, Luke was the one for me.

I was entering my formidable teenage years by 1981, I thought about Luke every day, I even took a picture that we had taken together and put it in a locket so that Luke would always be with me. A couple of mean teenage girls saw me reminiscing with the locket in my hand. One of the girls snatched it from my hand, started running with it and threw it over the school stairs. I rushed down the stairs to try and save it, but the locket had broken. "Why would you do that? That was my favorite locket, why would you do something like that?" I asked one of the girls, who I later found out was Tabitha McCoy. Tabitha replied; "because we felt like doing it, you freaking spaz!" I stood up from my chair in the hallway, and I punched Tabitha in the face, actually knocking her backwards and over the stairs. I didn't kill her, but she was badly hurt. Because of what that little witch did, I got suspended from school for a month. I tried to tell the principal what happened, but nobody wanted to listen to me, they just thought I was another troublemaker.

"Momma, please let me explain. She started it! She….." before I could finish, she stopped me. "I don't care if Moby Dick started the fight, you don't push someone down the stairs, Charlie. You need to go to that young girl's house and apologize!" I got so angry at my mother I blurted out two words that totaled seven letters. If you can figure it out, well, you must be a rocket scientist. I was beginning to develop a big attitude to go with my big hair. My mother asked me to repeat what I said, and like a dummy, I did just that. She then grabbed me by my hair, took me in the bathroom, wet some soap, and put it in my mouth. After sitting there for about 10 minutes with nasty tasting soap in my mouth, she took it out and asked if I was ready to apologize to Tabitha. I answered yes, and we walked on over to her house. When I rang the doorbell, Tabitha answered, she had two broken arms and two broken legs. "What do you want spaz, haven't you caused me enough pain?" Then before I could open my mouth, what she said took me by surprise.

"Before you say a word, I want to apologize to you. I shouldn't have made fun of you like that. It must be hard loving somebody that is so far away." I was shocked to hear this come from her. I apologized for my behavior  and after that we became the best of friends. Even though her popular cheerleader friends didn't like it. "Why would you want to become friends with that loser? Make your choice Tabatha, it's either her or us!" I was expecting Tabatha to drop me like a hot potato, but she didn't. She looked at her friends and she said; "look, I've now learned that everyone deserves friendship no matter where they come from, no matter what disability they have, no matter of anything, everybody deserves a friend. If you don't like it, well then we don't have to be friends anymore!" I apologized for making her lose the friendships that she had made, and she told me not to worry about it, she told me that if they couldn't accept the brand new Tabitha, then they didn't deserve to have her at all.

She informed me that a father/daughter dance was coming up at school soon. It was then I realized something, for the first time, I felt remorse for my father's death. When she spoke those words to me, I stared off into space for what must've been 10 seconds, but also apparently long enough to scare her into thinking I was having some sort of seizure or something of that sort. She must've called me 10 times, but I only heard the 10th call before snapping back to reality. "Where did you go my friend, is everything okay?" she asked, showing great concern. I told her that my dad had died a few years prior, and that I probably wouldn't go to the dance because I didn't have anyone to go with. That night when I went home after spending the day with Tabitha, I cried like a baby. I looked up to the heavens and apologized to my father for not saying goodbye properly. I felt something tap me on my shoulder and looked over. When I looked over, there was a man standing in front of me. "Hello, my darling, let me take a look at you. You know, you don't have to apologize to me, I should be apologizing to you. What I had done to you and the rest of the family was very wrong and I apologize."

We were able to give each other a hug, and just like that, he was gone. Tabitha had come over to play the next night. It was somewhere between May and June 1981, to have a sleepover with me, and we had a pretty in-depth conversation. We told each other everything including secret crushes . That's when I told her how special Luke was to me. She said that she once had a love like that. She said that his name was Sergio Del Monte and she had met him when her family was vacationing in Italy in the early part of 1978. "I loved him so much, I loved him with all of my heart and soul. Then we had to come back to the United States, I never saw him again." She wept. I gave her a hug, I told her that one day she would see Sergio again, just like one day I would see Luke again. She said she had an older brother, David, that would be happy to take me to the Father/daughter dance. I thought about this, but I politely declined. I declined because even though her brother was nice enough to offer to take me, he wasn't my father, and that will forever be reserved for him!

Her older brother, (age 19), begged and pleaded with me to go with him. I gave a huge sigh, to express non-interest, but he was a persistent little ass. Finally, after realizing my efforts to refuse him were futile, I agreed to go with him. "Don't worry, we will have the best time. When we got to the school, he led me into the gym doors by the hand. When we walked through the door, everyone stopped and stared. No one could believe that I was on the arm of such an attractive young man. All of the girls stared and swooned at the thought of being me. You see, David was the star running back of our football team, and one of the most eligible single men in our school. "So, you blew me off? You blew me off to go to a dance with this….. this…. this…. retard?" his former girlfriend, Rachel Tompkins said. I went to stand up, but he pushed me down with his hand against my chest and nodded his head no.

I could see Rachel and him going to the other side of the room, I couldn't make out what they were saying because they were too far away, but it ended with David getting a glass of punch thrown in his face. My guess is that she wanted him back, he said no and she threw a little hissy fit. "I'm so sorry about Rachel, she's just the jealous type, and you shouldn't have to deal with that. As we were dancing the night away, he dropped his arm around me and tried to pull me in for a kiss. "David, stop it! I told you I'm not interested in you like that, you need to respect that!" He apologized and offered to get me some punch. He came back with the punch and told me to drink up. I wondered why he smiled so widely, but I thought nothing of it. About five minutes after the punch had entered my system, I began to feel dizzy and very weird. I heard echoing voices; "come on, let's get you home." Even though I was half unconscious, I knew that we didn't go to my house. I knew David was planning to take advantage of me. I had something that he wanted, and I wouldn't give it to him willingly, so the only thing he knew to do was take it by force.

In the morning when I finally woke up, I woke up naked with my clothes strewn everywhere. He was sleeping next to me and I tried my best to escape his grasp. When I rolled over to exit the bed, I must've moved the mattress a little bit, because that's when he awoke. "Where the hell do you think you're going, to tell the police? I don't think so! You're not telling anyone anything!" Luckily for me, his sister had come upstairs and I ran to her. I told her what had happened, and she quickly called 911 and had him arrested. "David, I can't believe you would do that to my friend, my friend that I trusted you with. How could you do this to this family, how could you do this to her?" Tabatha asked him as he was being handcuffed. He tried apologizing to me and said it had just been a while since he has had sex and he just needed to release, but I didn't accept his apology. He took my innocence, and there's no apologizing for that.

Eventually he was charged with child abuse, child endangerment, sex with a minor, and having to register on Megan's Law. He was sentenced to 10 years in prison for what he had done to me. In my opinion, justice was not served. In my opinion, justice had eluded me, it wasn't fair. Tabitha took me into her home, showed me what it was like to really have a true friend that would care about me for the rest of my life. In 1985, Tabatha was engaged to be wed and invited me to be one of her bridesmaids. She got married on my 18th birthday. When I saw the groom, my mouth fell to the floor. The groom was Luke. When I asked how they met Tabatha smiled at me. "You poor little fool, he told me about your crush, and I decided to steal him. Don't you see, this was all part of my game! I have something you've always wanted, take a nice look!" I looked at Luke but he didn't even look at me. I don't think he remembered who I was, even when Tabatha evilly introduced him to me, there was no recollection of having known me at all.

"Luke, please, look at me. You can tell me you don't know me, what about all the good times we shared?" He looked at me for a second, and then he turned back to the wedding party. "Tabitha, I will never forgive you for this, you stole him from me and you know how wrong you were for doing that!" She just laughed at me, as if she didn't care. "Why don't you go away spaz girl, I don't need you for anything else!" Tabatha said, as she kicked me out of the party. I sat on the banquet hall stairs and cried. I couldn't believe that Tabitha would double cross me like that. A young man came up to me and asked me what was the matter, and I told him I didn't want to talk about it. When I looked up from my hands, I saw a young boy, brown wavy hair, cowboy boots, cowboy hat and standing about 6'2". "Come on my friend, you can tell me what's got you down." I told him about what Tabitha had done to me, and he wiped my tears away and just held me tight all through the night.

"You know, you don't even know me, why are you comforting me in this way?" I asked the strange man, hoping he would give me an answer. He didn't really answer me, and we just sat there in silence. I asked him his name and he said his name was Darwin, Darwin Brown. Darwin and his family were originally from Branson, Missouri but moved to Johnstown about a month ago. Darwin Brown was a black man, my mom didn't really approve of me dating outside of my own race. They were a little racist, but nice to Darwin's face. "I can't believe you would bring embarrassment to the family like this!" my mother said to me, trying to talk me out of dating a black man. "Look mama, I don't care what you say, I love Darwin, and I'm going to be with him. I'm 18 years old, and I can do what I want, and I don't even have to live here!" My mom kicked me out of the house and that was the end of that.

We got married on September 11, 1989, I didn't even invite my mom to the wedding because I knew they wouldn't approve. But about a week after we had gotten married, I got a nasty letter from my mom that basically said she  was disappointed in my choice to marry a black man, she was also disappointed that she wasn't even invited to the wedding. I gave birth to my daughter, Kelsey Marie, on August 4, 1991 at 8:58 AM. Darwin took a job as a mechanic, and I took a job as a hostess at Barney's Burger Hut. I was making seven dollars an hour, which at that time was pretty good money, and my husband made over 60,000 a year. We wanted nothing but the best for our daughter. Darwin was a high school dropout, so he was lucky to find a mechanic job, because everywhere else he applied required a degree.

My little butterbean was the perfect little girl. She didn't cry, she didn't fuss, she slept through the night since the day we brought her home. We have to leave her with a babysitter most hours of the day, and I hate it. I hate leaving my baby girl with a total stranger. Mrs. Anderson is a good old lady, she should be fine with her. September 9, 1991, I returned home from work to see my daughter's babysitter in a pool of blood. Someone had shot her numerous times, and no one knew why. Mrs. Anderson was 86 years old, and didn't have a single enemy. Who would want to kill this woman and why? Lo and behold, she was murdered by her own son for the insurance money that she had. He was arrested and charged that same day. Since her demise, it put me in a horrific position, because I knew that I couldn't take her to work with me, and I couldn't expect Darwin to quit his job.

"Honey, I don't know what we're going to do. I don't trust anyone with our daughter, and we don't have enough money to raise a child, not right now anyway." Darwin said to me while we were laying in bed for the night. "I don't know babe, maybe it's better if we......" Before I could say another word, he turned to me slowly and said, "we are not giving up our daughter for adoption, it's just not happening. But towards her first birthday of 1992, we couldn't take care of her anymore, and we put her in the foster care system. It broke my heart to have to put my daughter in foster care, but what was I supposed to do? She was only about a year old so it would be unlikely that she would remember us anyway. It's time we gave her to a loving family. I had never seen Darwin cry, but the day we dropped off Kelsey at the adoption center, Darwin cried like a baby. I tried not to cry, but after seeing his tears, I couldn't contain myself. I miss my daughter so much already, but this needed to be done.

Shortly after we decided to give Kelsey up for adoption, Darwin and I were always arguing and couldn't find a happy place. So we divorced on September 9, 1993. I was so distraught that I decided to move. Miami, Florida would be my new home, and I vowed that I would make many friends there. Darwin decided to stay in Johnstown. You might be wondering why I left my hometown, simply put, there was no emotional connection for me to Johnstown. Even when I was little, I never felt like I belonged over there. Miami was great, although I did have a hard time finding a new job, because nobody wanted to hire somebody with down syndrome. Most people, when I explain my disability, think that down syndrome means I will be fidgety and throw a tantrum when I don't get my way. Sure, there are some aspects of it where that might happen in some cases, but every case of down syndrome, or any other disability for that matter, is unique in its own way.

~ Let's break the fourth wall, and take you to the author, for example. The author writing this has cerebral palsy. He created me in his mind, he uses a wheelchair to get around, and he's a pretty awesome guy. I came from his brain. Some people with cerebral palsy, depending on the condition of cerebral palsy, some cerebral palsy can cause more brain damage due to lack of oxygen than others can. Anyway, enough about the author, back to my story. ~

I was out of work until 1995, if you can believe that. I collected unemployment for those two years. I didn't enjoy taking from the government, I hated it actually, but it had to be done. I finally got a job as a maid for a very wealthy family: Charles and Ashley Montague.

Charles and Ashley were nice people, their kids were little heathens though. They had two kids, and I took a special liking to one of them. Amber, I tcok a special liking to Amber because she had down syndrome just like me. We were able to bond better than anyone that she had to take care of her, because we understood each other. She was only four years old, but anytime I would walk through the door, her face would light up. One night, her mother confessed something to me: "You know, we are so glad that you have come into our lives. She loves you so much, how would you like to keep her full-time? We aren't trying to get rid of our daughter, but we just can't handle her." I found that sweet, but ultimately, I declined. I explained that I gave up my own daughter for adoption and felt horrible. I couldn't do that to somebody else. "Believe me, you would be doing us a favor, we can't take care of her anymore!" I asked her mother if it was the fact that she couldn't take care of Amber, or that she didn't want to take care of Amber, because there was a clear difference. "How dare you question the love I have for my daughter, you have no right!" she said, while getting quite defensive.

I told them I still can't do it; I told them I wouldn't do it. And then, I got to thinking, what kind of person would I be to let a little girl like that go into the foster care system? But then I thought, I was being hypocritical, because if I could save their child, why couldn't I save my own from the same fate? I, again, politely declined, and watched her go into the foster care system. It broke my heart, but I couldn't do it for one child and not my own flesh and blood. I tried to fight the Florida court system to get my daughter back, but they wouldn't let me have her back. They said that I would be unfit to be a mother because of my disability. They were worried about my mental state, and me not being able to take care of her the way her foster mother would. I threw a fit, a fit so great that they had to call security to escort me out of the building, and even threatened to have me arrested. I was going to show the Florida courts that I am a good mother, and that I deserve to have my daughter.

As time went on, I was able to talk to Kelsey and tell her everything that was going on. "Mom, I know you're trying to get me back and everything, but I don't want you back! I want to start a new life with a new family, I don't want to get to know you. You left me once, who's to say you won't do it again?" She said that to me one day as we were playing cards. I promised her that I would never hurt her like that again, and I asked her to please come home with me. When she said no a second time, that's when I knew my relationship with my daughter would be over. She wanted nothing to do with me, and honestly, I couldn't blame her. I was a train wreck, who would want to deal with me anyway? One day, while I was working, I happened to run into Tabitha. She looked at me and said; "Hello Charlie, it's been a while, how have you been?" To which I gave a salty reply; "you know what Tabitha? You can take those pleasantries and shove them up your tight little ass!"

Tabitha stood there with her mouth open, and I proceeded to take my index finger and close her mouth. "Oh there, isn't that better?" I said, in a smart ass tone. "What is wrong with you? I thought we were cool after my marriage to Luke. What did I do, why all of the hostility?" Tabitha asked me, with tears in her eyes. I felt remorse after being so mean to her. I quickly apologized and asked her how things were going with Luke. "Well, Charlie, if you really want to know I truly think that Luke and I are headed for divorce! Things just aren't working between us the way that they should be." I feel bad for Tabitha, but at the same time, I was thinking; "score, Luke shall be mine!" But then something called empathy came into my life; goodness I hate that bitch. I started to realize that I can't treat Tabitha like trash for something that Luke did. Luke had always known my feelings for him, he knew who I was at the wedding, I don't care what he says. Yet, he has managed to steal and break my heart once more.

I told him that he could have me anyway that he wanted. But like a gentleman, he declined. I wanted him to ravage me, pull me close, tell me that I was his only one. I wanted him to do a lot of things, but he never did. Yeah, I guess I could've taken what I wanted at that time that I had him bent over a barrel. But no, I decided not to do that to him. I couldn't hurt him again. Once Tabitha realized how strong my affection was for Luke, she filed for divorce in 2000. I think it was, yeah, sometime in 2000. I told her that she didn't have to do that, I told her that he was thinking about coming back. But nothing I could've said that evening would've made her turn around and come back into that building. I wish she had, because as she was backing out of a bar driveway, a speeding semi truck came up from behind and took out the back end of her Mazda. She then proceeded to spin around and go into the oncoming view of another tanker truck, the tanker truck is what killed her.

I was highly devastated, sure, I hated her for stealing my man, but I didn't want anything bad to happen to her. We  laid Tabitha to rest on December 17, 2000. I went to comfort Luke, but he still didn't want to pay attention to me. I wondered what I had done wrong. So I said I was done with him and had a nice conversation. "Luke, why have you been ignoring me all this time, why haven't you been talking to me?" He looked at me and said; "Because, I was starting to fall in love with you, and then you left me. I could never forgive you for that, I'm sorry!" I told him that I had no choice but to leave, I had to go with my mother! He turned away from me and went back to grieving over his beloved wife. I got him to go home with me, and we went to bed together. The next morning, he regretted it. "It was a mistake and it shall never happen again!" I asked him why, and he said because he didn't love me the way he thought he did. "I just thought it would be fun to have sex with somebody who has a disability, I wanted to see if you would be good at it."

"So, you just wanted my body? You wanted nothing to do with me?" After he turned away from me, I knew it was true, he never loved me, he just wanted the goods that came with me. I was devastated and vowed never to love again. But naturally, I have needs that need to be met, so I saw sex as a way of doing that. I was passed around more times than a turn-style when you go to an amusement park. I used a spermicide, plus birth control because I do not want to get pregnant again and have to make that difficult decision. It was hard enough with Kelsey, I don't know if I can do that again. In the later part of 2001, I want to say April or May of that year, I went against the Florida court system again to get my daughter back. And yet again, I was found mentally incompetent to take care of my own child. Listen, if I knew enough to have sex and have a baby, then I can almost guarantee you that I would be old enough to figure out how to take care of my daughter.

I left the Montague household in November 2001. I loved working for them, but I couldn't help but feel guilty because I had a hand in Amber being taken away. "Please don't leave, we need you here, you are a breath of fresh air!" Ms. Montague would beg me, but I told her I couldn't stay. I told her that I had to find some way to get my daughter back in my arms. "Well luckily for you, I am a lawyer. Ashley Montague, Attorney at Law. I will do this for you, pro bono. I've seen the way you've taken care of my daughter, there's no reason why you shouldn't have yours!" she said to me, as I went to give her a hug. "Thank you Ms. Montague, thank you! You really have no idea how much this means to me, oh my goodness, thank you, thank you, thank you!" On July 9th of that year, we went to Family Court to discuss all the reasons why I should have my little girl. I'm not going to bore you with all the legal details, but I did eventually get custody of Kelsey. She was now 10,so we had a lot of catching up to do.

We had a lot of fights, mostly because I was trying to be a mother, and she had no respect for my authority. Who could blame her though, she doesn't know me, so what reason would you have to listen to me? Just because I'm her mother? I can't expect a child, even though I gave birth to her, I can't expect a child to just warm up to me and listen to me. I suppose we tried our best to have a normal relationship, but it was hard. That is until 2003. 2003 is when we got really close. We got really close after her aunt and uncle had died in a car accident with my mother. My mother came out of the car accident unhurt, but my brother and sister weren't so lucky. "I am really going to miss them, it's not going to be the same without them!" Kelsey said to me. With a little knowledge, I decided to go to the University of Florida, and I decided to put a degree under my belt: Early Childhood Psychology. By 2008, I had graduated from the University of Florida.


Shortly after my graduation, I got a job at my daughters school as a counselor helping children sort out their problems. I was shocked to see one of my first patients was my own daughter. "Mama, you work here now? Great, now my social status will be ruined!" I told her to stop worrying about what people had to say about her, and to focus on schoolwork. "But mama, you don't understand, popularity is everything. If you are popular, everybody would do things for you. If you're not popular, you're just a nerd and I refuse to be a nerd!" I couldn't believe Kelsey was behaving this way, not my little girl. She explained to me that three girls were picking on her because of me. When I asked why they would make fun of her because of me, she said that the girls were calling me nothing but a retard and everything. She said it took everything inside of her not to punch all three girls in the face.

One night, I was celebrating with some friends at a bar for a friend of mine's birthday; we had some heavy drinks and we partied all night. We all drove separately that night for whatever reason, and that proved not to be such a great idea. As I was walking to my car, I heard footsteps come up behind me, and before I knew it, there was a knife at my throat, and gun at my back. "Don't move little lady, you do exactly as we say, and no one will get hurt." one of the men said to me. There were two men and a woman, at least what I can assume is a woman because it was dark, and all I saw was a long ponytail. So, who really knows what I saw that night, but I know that it was the scariest night of my life. I tried to scream, but no one was around to hear me…or so I thought. A man came out of nowhere to defend my honor. He smelt like pee and bad cheese. He was a homeless man, his name was Gerard Higgins. After he saved my life, Mr. Higgins and I got to talking.

As it turns out, Mr. Higgins was a man who served in the Iraq war, and suffered from PTSD. He tried getting help from medical professionals, but no one would help him without the proper insurance. "The US really dropped the ball when it comes to taking care of our veterans, there's no way that you should live like this, Mr. Higgins." I said to him, and he politely agreed. "Yes, it appears that the US Army has really dropped the ball on me. Do you know how cold the winter nights are here? I would give anything for a warm bed and somewhere inside to have a warm cooked meal." I felt bad for him, so I invited him to stay with me. He looked at me to see if I was joking, but I wasn't. I wanted to thank him for all that he had done for me that night. "Ma'am, I appreciate your offer, but I would not want to impose." I told him not to be silly and that it would be my honor to have him as a guest. I told him that I still had some of my fathers old clothes if he wanted to come home with me and take a shower and get a nice hot meal.

I led him to my car, and we went home. Luckily it was a nice day, so I could leave the windows open in the car. Not trying to be mean or anything, but his stench was almost unbearable. Once we pulled into my driveway and I let him out, I cleaned out my car immediately. Again, I know it's not his fault, but I didn't want my car to smell like the back of a garbage truck forever. When he undressed, I watched him shower. Not because I found him sexually Interesting in anyway, but because this was a stranger in my home, and I wanted to make sure that he didn't steal anything. I know, I know, that is very wrong to say of our men and women in uniform. But what was I supposed to say or do? He was 36 years old, and I was 35. I wasn't expecting to fall in love that day, but I did.

When he emerged from the shower, his body was dripping wet, and I saw a side of him that I didn't see in the alleyway where I almost got abducted. When he emerged from the shower, I saw him as somebody that I wanted to be with for the rest of my life. A musclebound, 6'8" black man, who was very well to do in the nether region, but we're not going to go into great detail; this is not the kind of book. Needless to say, we made love that night, and it was heavenly. Kelsey wasn't too thrilled about me bringing a stranger into our home, "mommy, what if he's an ax murderer? Do you know anything about this man? What if he tells his buddies that we live here?" I told her to stop being paranoid and that everything would be okay. I gave Mr. Higgins a job as my secretary at Kelsey's school. He was so grateful for the opportunity that he gave me a kiss on the cheek. "Thank you, thank you for giving me a second chance to live again!"

I told him that he was very welcome and that I would do anything for him within reason. There was something about Mr. Higgins that I didn't know. Mr. Higgins was homeless indeed, but what he didn't tell me is that he was guilty of more than 16 murders in his 36 years of life. Once I found this out, I kicked him out faster than his head could ever spin. "But, babe, you have to believe me, I have changed!" I wanted to believe him, but at the same time I couldn't believe him, not with a young daughter. She was about 12 years old, and I didn't want her growing up with a murderer for a step-father. I kicked him out and I didn't see him again for three or four years. It was either 2006 or 2007 when I saw him again. "Excuse me ma'am, can you spare a….. oh it's you, what do you want? Come here to kick me down a few more pegs?" I apologized to him for what I had done, and I offered my home to him again.

"If I come back to stay with you, how do I know you're not gonna yank my home right out from under me?" I told him I didn't know, all I knew was that he would have to learn to trust me, and that I was truly sorry for the way I treated him. It began to rain so I hurried him to my car, but he didn't move. "I'm not going anywhere with you, I would rather stay in the streets than be teased with a home and home cooked meal when you don't even really mean it!" I explained to him that I never meant to hurt him that way, that I was just looking out for my daughter. He let out a huge sigh and said he forgave me for what I had done. "You know, I understand, hearing that a man is convicted of 16 murders is a hard pill to swallow, and I get that. But, please know that it was a part of my life that I left behind in my early teens, and I would never do that to anyone again." I looked at him because I was unsure of his newfound sincere attitude. "Momma, you let him in here again? How could you, don't you care about my safety?" Of course I cared about my daughter's safety, I told her that if he slipped up even once, he would be out.

"Once, once?! What is the one time that you give him a chance he uses it to murder me? Huh, what about that?" I told her to stop worrying about that, that Mr. Higgins was a good guy who was just down on his luck. Kelsey mumbled something under her breath, but when I asked her to repeat it, she didn't, so I'm guessing that it was something not so nice to our house guest. I at least owed him a room and three home-cooked meals after he saved my life. I could be laying in a ditch right now, but thanks to Mr. Higgins, I am not. "Mom, I do not approve of this! Please have him removed from our house, please mama, please mama, please mama, please!" I understood how uncomfortable it made my daughter, but I also understood that Mr. Higgins had nowhere to go. I was under quite the dilemma, even though my decision should've been obvious. Mr. Higgins hadn't done anything to my daughter since she started staying with us, so I had no reason not to trust him around my daughter, therefore, I didn't kick him out.

"So, you have made your decision. I see how much I mean to you, mom. You never loved me at all, you just love the fact that you can have a man in your pants every day of the week." she said to me, packing her bags. "Kelsey, you're not going anywhere! You are in my house, and you will follow my rules. The company I keep in this house is of no concern to you! Do I make myself clear?" Where does your daughter go when she can't talk to you because you're an idiot and choose a criminal over your daughter? I will tell you where she goes, she goes to CPS and tells them that I am dating a rapist and murderer. I admitted that I was dating someone I knew to be a convict from the law, but I knew nothing of the rape charges. "I tried to make that up to make him a worse off human being." Kelsey said to me, while laughing. Kelsey got what she wanted and she was removed from my possession once again. I just wanted to cry, but I took up drugs instead. I went hard-core into heroine and would do things for guys that I can't even speak of. I am sure you are thinking to yourself; "a girl with down syndrome couldn't possibly get into this much trouble, could she?"

When I was done with my heroin phase, I quickly went into crack cocaine, and other things of that nature. Always remember, just because I am a person with a disability, doesn't mean that my life will differ from anyone else's, depending on the situation. I was in a bad way. If you are thinking; "I've never seen a drug addict down syndrome girl, would that even exist?" Well, if you have met me, I'm probably the first or one of very few that have this problem. I struggled with drugs until 2011 when I decided that enough was enough, and I needed to get clean. I needed to do better. I stayed in a halfway house until the beginning of 2013 before being released back into the public population. Kelsey was outside waiting for me. I was getting ready to celebrate my 45th year of life. My daughter let me stay with her until I got back on my feet. I moved away from Florida, but Kelsey had really grown accustomed to Florida, and wanted to make something of herself there. I was going to miss my daughter, but we needed to go separate ways now. I gave her a hug goodbye, and I left for my new place of living: Nashville, Tennessee.

I started working at a karaoke bar. I would even take my turn at singing every Tuesday night. I really love country music, so that's something I would always sing. I always got standing ovations when I sang, however, I just thought it was people being nice to me. I sound like a dying cow, but to these people, I sound like an angel? I don't get it, I really don't. "You should try out for "Texas has talent" the TV show. I think you would really do great on that show." my manager, Bobby Lockhart, said to me. I blew him off. I didn't think I had what it takes, and I didn't want to set myself up for failure. But they do always say, you fail at 100% of the shots you don't take. I decided to go on the show and I sang my little heart out.  After I was done singing, the judges had tears in their eyes, and I could look all around the auditorium and everybody was standing and cheering for me. One of the judges, Carmen Jessup, pressed the platinum buzzer, which meant that I was automatically going to the next round.

At the age of 45, I was knocking young kids out of the competition. Kids that thought they would have no problem beating me. I ended up winning the whole competition, and went under a new alias as a country star. My name is now Lena Lester. Under that name, I recorded my first song "Don't Go Standing on My Foot". It was at number one for 35 weeks in a row. People really loved the song, and I made more money from that song than I had ever dreamed of. in 2013, I released my first album titled "Cut Me Deeper". The album "Cut Me Deeper" debuted at number one for another 26 weeks. I was one of the most successful country stars for my age, especially for a country star who was up-and-coming. I got to be featured on many famous music stars' albums. I finally felt like I was in a good place. It was then that I got a call from Luke, wanting to see me. First I was hesitant, I had thought maybe that he had just wanted to see me because of all the money I was making.

"No, no absolutely not. I realized how much I loved you, I have always loved you, I've just been too afraid to show it!" he said. I wanted to believe him, but I was understandably skeptical. We met up at a local diner and had some coffee. After our coffee and dessert, he kissed me passionately. The years have not been kind to him. He looks like an old, withered, leather bag. Oddly enough though, I still loved him. I have always loved him. I would take him with me everywhere I traveled - Nashville, Pittsburgh, Orlando, Miami, Colorado, you name it, I've been there. I enjoyed all the sights and sounds of each city that I had gone to. My favorite city was New Orleans. I loved all the crawfish and excellent cuisine. I was in heaven and didn't want to leave. So I did it, I bought a mansion in New Orleans, Louisiana, and made it my permanent residence. From Johnstown, to Florida, to Texas, now I'm in New Orleans. My life couldn't get any better than it is right now!"

Now I found myself in a conundrum, because I loved Luke, and I always have. The problem was Gerard has come into my life and I love him too. Do I go with the one who I have always loved since I was a child, or do I give the new one a try? That was my dilemma  and I didn't know how to face it, so I had called Kelsey for her advice. "Look, mom, I'm sorry you're going through this hard time, but I can't help you. I told you how I felt about Mr. Higgins, and you ignored me. Now you can deal with this alone." Two years later I was still having second thoughts. Around that time I was also diagnosed with alopecia. My hair was falling out and I felt like the ugliest woman on the face of the planet. One man grew closer to me, while the other one slowly drifted away from me. Can you guess which one did what? The results may surprise you. It was Mr. Higgins that started backing away from me.


"I'm sorry, Charlie. I can't be with a woman who has no hair. It's just not my style!" Mr. Higgins said to me. I was shocked about this because of everything I had done for him. I guess some people are just ungrateful. I couldn't believe Mr. Higgins was acting this way. I thought we had a good connection. I thought he really loved me, but I guess I was wrong. Along with my alopecia, I started hacking up a lung in the middle part of 2015. Luke urged me to get checked after putting it off until May of that year. I got tested for breast cancer, and a couple days later, I found out that's indeed what I have. It was with that, that Luke had left me as well. "I can't deal with having a sick girlfriend, I have my own life to worry about. I can't worry about you all the time!" I couldn't believe he would say that to me. I couldn't believe he would leave somebody dying and alone, but that's exactly what he did.

I called my daughter to tell her of my cancer diagnosis. She said she felt bad, but she wouldn't be able to come and take care of me. She has her own family now, and didn't have time for me. "Kelsey, please. I'm begging you, please come and help me." She said no and hung up the phone. I couldn't believe that I was sick and alone. My whole entire life, I never dreamed that this would happen to me. I felt really alone and that's when I started talking to God a lot more. I would talk to Him every day. I found a church that was very accepting of me, and I actually became a pastor and delivered sermons every Sunday. Many people loved me. It was with my church community that I had received tons of donations for my chemotherapy treatments. That's when I saw him, a young man by the name of Derek Mason. Derek was a regular at my sermons. Originally an atheist, I was able to turn him around to see the Light of God.

We fell in love, and I married Derek in 2017. In 2017 I had spent that year in remission from my cancer. I always feared that the cancer would come back, so I repeatedly asked the congregation to pray for me that the cancer wouldn't come back. Unfortunately, in 2019 the cancer did come back, but this time it was much worse. This time they only gave me six months to a year to live. I called my daughter again with the horrific news. Despite all of this, she still didn't want to see me. "Momma, what part of this aren't you understanding? I want nothing to do with you! Are we clear?" I told her we were crystal clear and that I wouldn't bother her again. She said that was good and we hung up the phone. I couldn't believe my own daughter was so cold towards me, although maybe this is what I deserve for not listening to her when it came to Mr. Higgins.

I felt like my whole world was crashing down. Luke left me, Mr. Higgins left me, my own daughter doesn't even want to talk to me. What kind of human being must I be to have alienated everyone around me? During the summer of 2018, things were getting really bad. My hair was falling out rapidly, and I couldn't keep anything down as far as food goes. Finally, I got a strange knock on my door. When I opened it, I was shocked to see Kelsey standing there. "Hello, mother. Do you know you're lucky I'm here? I was thinking about leaving you today on your own, but then I thought better of it." she said to me. This wasn't exactly reassuring, but it was better than having no one and being all alone. I was amazed at how well Kelsey could take care of me. It turns out, she was a registered nurse at a local hospital in Johnstown, Pennsylvania. I told her I was so proud of her and all of her accomplishments. "Wait, you're proud of me? I've never heard you say that in my whole entire life! What's going on?"

"What are you talking about? You're my daughter, of course I would be proud of you no matter what you did! I may not say it to you. But I love you and I'm very proud of you!" My daughter and my new husband decided to take care of me at home. There was an option to keep me in the hospital and possibly move into hospice, but if I was going to die, I wanted to die in the comfort of my own home with my family. (cough, cough, cough, cough) Oh my goodness, excuse me, these chemotherapy treatments take a lot out of me. Anyway, I proceeded to do my sermons every Sunday, until one Sunday, I fell very ill and collapsed in the middle of a sermon. Thank heavens for the quick thinking of my congregation, otherwise I don't think I would've made it. When I opened my eyes I was in the hospital and Kelsey was standing next to me. "Oh mom, thank goodness you're all right, thank goodness you are still here with me. I'm sorry for what I had said before, you mean the world to me and I couldn't imagine losing you!"

"Couldn't imagine losing me? Last week you just said that you hoped I would die and that you never wanted to see or talk to me again. Now, you're happy that I'm alive?" I asked, skeptical of my daughter's real intentions. "Mama, I swear, my intentions to you are nothing but good. I swear on the hands of God." Luke came to see me, but I quickly turned him away. "If you didn't want me at my worst, then you don't deserve me at my best!" Things got so bad for me that I had to cancel most of my tour dates for 2018. Many people left hurtful messages on community message boards for me. I could understand why people were upset because they bought the tickets, and now I'm not coming, but that's no reason to threaten my life. "Pay no mind to them mama, they are just angry fans. They really don't wish you ill will." In 2018, for the second time, I again achieved remission, and was able to go back to my lifestyle of which I had become accustomed to.

In 2018, I was performing a concert in Los Angeles, California. I got really dizzy and fell to the stage floor. I must've fallen pretty hard, because when I came through in the hospital, I had a walnut on my head the size of the Empire State building. Okay, so that's a bit of an exaggeration, but I do have a nice size bump and gash on my head. When I had asked doctors what was going on, they said that the cancer had come back, and it would not be operable this time. It was too far in my system to be operated on. I had to cancel my tours for the rest of 2018 and 2019. This didn't sit well with my loyal fan base. I was receiving death threats online and everything, if I didn't perform my shows . But I couldn't perform my shows, I was way too sick. Despite my money and wealth, money was dwindling and I couldn't afford my treatments. The doctors said they couldn't put me on a payment plan or anything like that, that I needed the money up front and I need it now. Otherwise, my path to death will be a lot faster

I was scared, but at the same time, I was relieved. I was relieved that my fight with cancer might be over soon, relieved that I wouldn't have to put up with the daily stresses of life, and relieved that I can finally see my brother and sister again. I saw my mother one last time in 2020 during the pandemic, she ended up catching COVID-19 and dying from those complications. Me? Well, I'm just hanging on day by day, trying to make the best of a bad situation. It is summertime here. I don't get to go out and enjoy the sun much, because I just don't feel like getting out of bed half the time. My mother died on October 19, 2020, at the age of 82. I was devastated. I was devastated and couldn't even make it to the funeral due to my condition. Somebody was able to share a live video of her funeral service, but it wasn't the same. I wanted to be there for my mother, I wanted to be there for everyone in my family during this time, and it hurt that I couldn't be.

As a matter of fact, and I'm telling you this story in 2022, I landed in the hospital again because my cancer keeps coming back. Things don't look good for me this time. I think I have defied the odds and gone long enough. It's time for me to accept my fate and go up to heaven. Like I said, it's summertime here, but I can't really go outside. I'm too weak. I'm too weak to stand; I'm too weak to do anything. I guess in a small way, you can say I'm wasting summer's breath, because I'm not getting out and enjoying it. But you know what, I've had a pretty good life. I've had many love interests in my life. I have a good daughter, and I think I've done pretty alright with life in general. When God calls me home, I truly believe I am ready to go home and be with my brother, sister, father, and mother, and we can all be a happy family once more. That's one thing I wish I could've changed, being kinder to my father when he was around. Well, I guess I can't change it now. I'm going to get some rest and I will talk to you guys later (beep, beep, beep, beep, beep, beep, beep……..)

As you may have noticed by those beeps, on June 19, 2022, Charlie Manson lost her battle with breast cancer at the age of 54. She died peacefully in her sleep at around 1:15 PM that day. She died surrounded by her husband, daughter, and a host of friends and family. Her contributions to country music in the ward will never be forgotten. Her smile has graced our presence in life, just as it will in death. Daughter, mother, pastor, and most importantly, friend. Those are all the words that you could use to describe Charlie Manson. She leaves behind a daughter and granddaughter. She leaves behind a lot more than that, though. She leaves behind a legacy that will never be touched by anyone. Anyone who was looking enough to know Charlie, is lucky enough to have her in their lives.

Dedication

This book is hereby dedicated to every person out there fighting their own battles and continuing to fight the good fight. It is because of you that I am able to write books like this. If you are disabled or have cancer, or any life-threatening disease like Charlie had, I want you to keep fighting. Sure, sometimes it's almost unbearable, but I want you to keep fighting. Sure, Charlie fought a lengthy battle and lost, but she still stood her ground and made the best of whatever she could do. You can too, even when hope seems bleak. Just know that you have all the power in the world to fight, and that there will always be a support system there with our Lord and Savior. May this book resonate with you forever and always. God bless you all.

www.ingramcontent.com/pod-product-compliance
Lightning Source LLC
Chambersburg PA
CBHW080730120726
48001CB00010B/3187